Just Grace Gets Crafty

s Crafty

Written and illustrated
by

# Charise Mericle Harper

HOUGHTON MIFFLIN HARCOURT
Boston   New York

www.hmhco.com

The text of this book is set in Dante MT.
The illustrations are pen-and-ink drawings digitally colored in Photoshop.

*The Library of Congress has cataloged the hardcover edition as follows*:
Harper, Charise Mericle.
Just Grace gets crafty / by Charise Mericle Harper.
p. cm.
Summary: "There's a new crossing guard in town named Marie who needs
a bit of help making friends, a fun substitute teacher for Miss Lois, and most
exciting, Grace and Mimi are going to have their own table at a craft fair."
—Provided by publisher.
[1. Best friends—Fiction. 2. Friendship—Fiction. 3. Handicraft—Fiction.]
I. Title.
PZ7.H231323Juq 2014
[Fic]—dc23
2013038995

ISBN: 978-0-544-08023-2 hardcover
ISBN: 978-0-544-58237-8 paperback

Manufactured in the United States of America
DOC 10 9 8 7 6 5 4 3 2 1
4500559330

For my Just Grace fans: I didn't think I could write more than one of these books, and now I've written twelve. Never give up—you might surprise yourself too.

# ABOUT ME IN 205 WORDS
### (not including comics)

1. My name is Grace, but my teacher, Miss Lois, calls me Just Grace. It all happened because there are three other Graces in my class. Miss Lois said, "Four Graces is too confusing," and then she made each of us use the first letter of our last name as part of our new Grace name. Grace Landowski was not happy with her new name, Grace L., but when a teacher says something, you pretty much have to go along with it. When it was my turn for a new name, I said, "Since no one else is using just Grace, can I be called just Grace?" Miss Lois wasn't paying very good attention, because she wrote down Just Grace instead of only the Grace part, and then I was stuck with it.

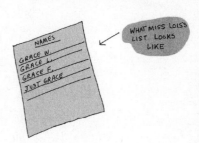

NAMES

GRACE W.
GRACE L.
GRACE F.
JUST GRACE

← WHAT MISS LOIS'S LIST LOOKS LIKE

2. My best friend, Mimi, lives right next door to me.

3. I have a dog named Mr. Scruffers, but she is a girl dog. When you adopt a dog, you sometimes have to keep the name they come with. This is what happened to me.

4. I have a teeny-tiny superpower. No one can see it, because it is a feeling power.

5. I like to draw, and sometimes I even make comics.

# THINGS THAT ARE EXCITING

Not everyone is excited about the same things. People are excited about all kinds of different things, and sometimes you will be surprised at what they can be excited about.

SAMMY →

DID YOU KNOW THAT ANIMAL POOP IS CALLED SCAT?

THERE ARE EVEN PEOPLE WHO STUDY ANIMAL POOP. ISN'T THAT AMAZING?

But the biggest surprise of all is when you surprise your very own self. That's what happened to me when Mom said, "Guess what? There's going to be a new crossing guard down on Blaine Avenue." "Is it for us?" I asked. Mom nodded, and then a second later I jumped up and high-fived the air. Normally

I wouldn't be excited about a crossing guard, but this was a special crossing guard, a crossing guard that Mimi and I were going to use every single day—two times. It was almost like a present. The crossing guard meant we wouldn't have to walk an extra two blocks to get to school. To someone else that might not seem like a very big change, but to us it was huge!

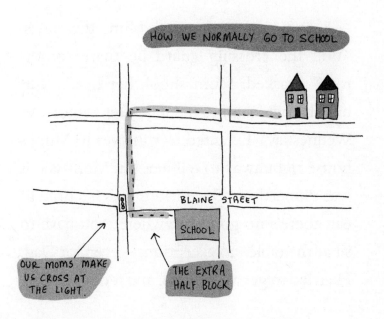

HOW WE NORMALLY GO TO SCHOOL

BLAINE STREET

SCHOOL

OUR MOMS MAKE US CROSS AT THE LIGHT.

THE EXTRA HALF BLOCK

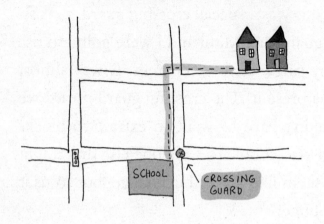

THE NEW WAY TO GET TO SCHOOL

SCHOOL

CROSSING GUARD

I couldn't wait to tell Mimi the news. "Will the crossing guard be there tomorrow?" I asked. Mom shook her head. "But he'll be here soon—the day after tomorrow, Wednesday." I wanted to run over to Mimi's house right away to tell her, but Mom said it was dinnertime. Once Mom says it's time to eat, there's no going anywhere. You have to sit at the table, no exceptions—even for Dad. He tried to get away once, and it didn't work.

Mom is kind of bossy when it comes to meals. The only family member who doesn't have to sit at the table is Mr. Scruffers, my dog. When we first got her, I had the idea to take a picture of her sitting at the table like she was eating with us. I was lucky that I snapped the photo before Mom came into the room, because her feelings about my idea were not the same as mine. She does not like dogs sitting at the table, especially if she sees them trying to lick the plates. Mr. Scruffers is smart—as soon as Mom shouted out her name, she jumped off the chair and ran to hide in the living room.

During dinner Mr. Scruffers usually sits under the table, by our feet, while we eat, but after Mom yelled at her, she stayed in the living room hiding for the whole meal. I think Mom had guilty feelings about that, because she saved a little piece of her hamburger on her plate, and when we were all done eating, she gave it to Mr. Scruffers as a treat. Normally Mr. Scruffers doesn't get treats from the table—at least, treats Mom knows about.

THE TABLE

MY HAND GIVING MR. SCRUFFERS SOME FOOD FROM MY PLATE

## THE SURPRISE AT DINNER

I wasn't hungry for dinner because I was thinking too much about the crossing guard, and how surprised Mimi was going to be when she found out the news. Sometimes when you are really excited about something, the excitement can fill your whole stomach up like a giant balloon and then there's no room left over for food. That's what was happening to me. This was not good, because Mom is also bossy about finishing your dinner. Right now I was wishing for one of two things, but the bad part was that they were both impossible. Even though my brain knew that, I kept on wishing for them—a superpower or a magic wand.

THE SUPERPOWER
OF RUNNING REALLY
FAST, SO I COULD RUN
TO THE KITCHEN WITH
MY FULL PLATE, EMPTY IT,
AND THEN COME BACK
AND SIT AT THE TABLE,
AND NO ONE WOULD SEE
ME DO IT.

FAST LEGS

A MAGIC WAND,
SO I COULD MAKE
THE FOOD ON MY
PLATE DISAPPEAR.

MAGIC
WAND

I tried to make a plan in case my wish didn't come true, but it's not easy to make a plan when you have only a few minutes of thinking time before you have to use it.

But suddenly my problem was solved, because right in front of me was Mom's special chicken—the kind that is my favorite, with the homemade crispy coating. Instantly the excitement bubble popped and my stomach was hungry. It was the second surprise of the night. If I kept getting surprised by the things I was doing, pretty soon I'd be like a stranger in my own body.

# WHAT HAPPENED AFTER DINNER

I raced straight over to Mimi's house. I knocked on the door and then stuck my hand through the mail slot and waved it around.

Suddenly someone grabbed my hand and started pulling. "AAHHHHH!" I screamed, and I tried to pull it back out, but I was trapped. And then I heard laughing. It was Mimi's little brother, Robert. I pulled and screamed at him to let go, but he wouldn't. I yelled for Mimi—"MIMI, HELP! HELP!"—but nothing happened. She couldn't hear me. The only thing to do was to try to ring the doorbell, so someone would hear it and come and save me.

# WHO SAVED ME

Robert was lucky that it was Mimi who came to the door. She got mad at him, but not as mad as his mom or dad would have been. Even though she was really nice to me and apologized, I think she thought it was kind of funny. When you have a best friend, you can sometimes tell what they are thinking even if they don't say anything.

Mimi told me to come in, but I couldn't wait until we were inside—I told her the news, right then. That's why we ended up sitting on her doorstep—we couldn't wait to talk about it. It was a nice place to sit, and for a second I thought about how it was kind of strange that we'd never sat there before. When something is new and different, it's hard not to notice it. But I didn't have any time to think about it, not after what happened next.

## WHAT HAPPENED NEXT

Sammy Stringer walked by and saw us sitting on Mimi's front step.

## SAMMY STRINGER DESCRIBED IN THIRTY WORDS

- Likes strange things.
- Is friends with my next-door neighbor Mrs. Luther.
- Is best friends with Max.
- Is friends with me and Mimi.
- Is scared of cats.
- Is very unusual.

As soon as Sammy saw us he waved, and then he checked the yard to make sure that Crinkles, Mrs. Luther's cat, wasn't around. Sammy is not a fan of Crinkles. If he were a superhero, cats would be the way to totally defeat him. Just thinking about that made me smile. It was good Sammy couldn't see my thoughts. To him, it just looked like I was happy to see him.

I'm not always super happy to see Sammy Stringer. It's not that I don't like him—it's just that talking to him is not always easy. He doesn't think the same way other people do, so understanding him takes up more energy. It's like he could be part alien or something. Not the scary-creature part of being an alien, but the being-from-a-different-planet part.

# WHY I WAS HAPPY TO SEE SAMMY STRINGER

I couldn't wait to tell him about the crossing guard. Having exciting new news is fun, but the best part about news is getting to tell other people about it. I didn't say anything until Sammy was standing right in front of us, and then I told him about the crossing guard.

# THE BIG SURPRISE FOR ME

Sammy already knew all about it, but that wasn't the biggest surprise. The biggest surprise was that Sammy had news for us! "Did you hear about Miss Summers?" asked Sammy. "She's coming for a week." Both Mimi and I shook our heads. What was Sammy talking about? This is how things work with Sammy—everything he says is confusing. "She's supposed to be really nice," he said. Mimi and I looked at each other and shrugged, and then Mimi asked the question that needed to be asked. "Who is Miss Summers?" Sammy looked at us like he'd never heard such a crazy question. He shook his head. "She's the substitute teacher while Miss Lois is away." Miss Lois had never mentioned one word about going away. Mimi and I both spoke at the same time.

Sammy nodded and smiled.

# WHAT SAMMY TOLD US IN THIRTY WORDS

- Miss Lois is going away for a teacher convention.
- She will be gone for a week.
- Miss Summers is going to be our substitute teacher.
- Mrs. Luther told him everything.

Mimi and I had lots of questions, but Sammy didn't have any of the answers.

Suddenly Sammy pointed to something behind us and said, "There's a hand over there." Before I could say anything, my brain made a picture of what he had said. It was not a nice picture to think about.

WHAT I WAS THINKING.

HAND IN THE BUSHES

It was a relief to turn around and see that the hand belonged to someone—Robert. He was sticking his hand out the mail slot and waving it around. It was the exact same thing that I'd done—only he was inside and I had been outside. "You should grab it," whispered Mimi. "Hang on to it like he did to you. Teach him a lesson." I shook my head. I had a better idea. I looked around the yard for something to use, and then saw a small garden shovel. I ran over, grabbed it, and scooped up some dirt.

## WHO CAN SCREAM LOUDER THAN ANY OTHER CREATURE ON EARTH?

Robert!

## WHO USUALLY GETS IN TROUBLE IF ROBERT YELLS?

Mimi.

## WHO GOT IN TROUBLE THIS TIME?

Me!

Mimi's mom is not the kind of mom who likes dirt all over the floor, and that's exactly what happened when Robert pulled his hand back through the mail slot. That, and lots of screaming. I apologized, but what helped more was when I said I'd clean it up. Parents like that kind of thing. It's called being responsible for your actions. Normally cleaning up dirt wouldn't be fun, but Mimi's mom has one of those cool robot vacuum cleaners, so this was different. Even Sammy stayed around, because it's not every day that you get to play with a robot—even if it's a cleaning robot.

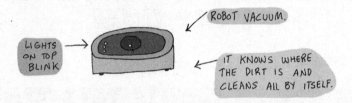

LIGHTS ON TOP BLINK

ROBOT VACUUM.

IT KNOWS WHERE THE DIRT IS AND CLEANS ALL BY ITSELF.

# SAMMY'S IDEA

Sammy staying turned out to be good, because he had the great idea to make the dirt into a path. That way we could make the vacuum go wherever we wanted. We made lots of different paths, and even had to get more dirt.

ROBOT VACUUM FOLLOWS THE PATH

THE EXTRA DIRT WE PUT ON THE GROUND TO MAKE A FUN PATH.

Sammy said it was too bad that it wasn't nighttime, because taping glow sticks on the vacuum would have looked super cool. I could tell that he was hoping that Mimi would say something like *Great idea, come back tonight and we'll do it,* but she didn't. Instead she said, "It's a good thing my mom's upstairs with Robert. She has lots of rules about the vacuum." It was longer than a no, but it meant the same thing.

After a while, even a super-cool robot vacuum can get kind of boring, so Sammy left and Mimi and I put it away. I was about to invite Mimi over to my house, but then my mom called and said it was close to bedtime. Sometimes when you are having fun, you can forget that it is a school night.

BYE, MIMI. SEE YOU TOMORROW.

ME RUNNING HOME

That night before bed, Mimi and I flashed our lights on and off for each other. Mimi's bedroom is right across from my bedroom, so we can see each other doing it. We do it almost every single night, and I don't know about Mimi, but I don't always think of the same three words when I flash my lights. Tonight I made up something new.

# WHO WOKE UP EXTRA EARLY

ME! The Miss Summers mystery made me want to get to school right away. This was not a usual thing. Even if you like something, it does not always mean you want to do it five days in a row. That's how I feel about school. I like it, but four days would be better. Mimi must have felt the same as me about Miss Summers, because she got to my house extra early. We walk to school together every day—it's our tradition. Mom let us go ten minutes early because I told her we were going to walk slow since it was our last time walking this route. Tomorrow the new crossing guard would be working and we'd go a different way. Last things are not like first things. Everyone remembers first things, but unless you pay extra attention, last things happen without you even noticing them until they are gone, and then it's too late.

All the way to school, Mimi and I paid special attention to everything. We wanted to remember this walk forever. "Let's do this on the way home too," said Mimi. "That way we can have a coming and going memory." I nodded. It was a good idea.

## WHAT WE FOUND OUT ABOUT MISS SUMMERS WHEN WE GOT TO SCHOOL

Nothing. No one knew anything about Miss Lois going away. If I didn't know that Sammy always told the truth, I would have been suspicious of his story. There are some kids that like to make stuff up, but Sammy isn't like that. If he says something is true, then it probably is true. I hoped that the Miss Summers thing wasn't supposed to be a secret, because by the time the bell rang to go inside, everyone knew about it. It made us all excited to get to class. What would she look like? Was she old like Miss Lois, or was she young? Did she shout and yell? Was she going to make us do our regular work? Were we going to study desert homes like Miss Lois said? If we'd wanted to, we could have probably come up with a million questions. But the question I most wanted the answer to was this one:

WILL SHE BE NICE, LIKE SAMMY SAID SHE WAS?

# WHAT YOU CAN SOMETIMES TELL ABOUT SOMEONE JUST BY LOOKING AT THEM

This is not always true, but it was true for me that day. The moment I saw Miss Summers, I knew I was going to like her. She was young, she had brown hair, and, best of all, she had a friendly smile. Not all smiles are friendly, so that part was important.

MISS SUMMERS WEARING HER FRIENDLY SMILE.

## SMILES THAT ARE NOT GOOD

TEETH TOO POINTY

UNCOMFORTABLE SMILE

GIANT FAKE SMILE

EVIL VILLAIN SMILE

The first thing Miss Summers said was that she was going to be our substitute teacher while Miss Lois was at a teachers' convention. Even though we all knew that, we were mostly polite and pretended like we didn't. There were two exceptions—Owen 1 and Robert Walters, but that was no surprise. They both like to make trouble.

A regular substitute teacher would have probably ignored them, but Miss Summers was not a regular teacher. She made Robert Walters and Owen 1 stand up at the front, and then while they stood there, she dragged their desks so that they were right next to hers—one on each side. I thought she might be angry, but instead of seeming mad she was super happy. It was not what any of us was expecting—especially not Owen 1 or Robert Walters.

# WHAT WAS SURPRISING AND GOOD

Miss Summers said that instead of working on learning about the desert, we were going to be doing a creative writing project. At first, I was worried about that. When Miss Lois got back she was going to be angry. I could already imagine it.

I felt a lot better after Miss Summers said, "I talked this over with Miss Lois, and she said that the desert project is one of her favorites. So we decided to leave that until she gets back. That way she can do it with you."

Not everyone in the class was excited about creative writing, but I was. I love making up stories almost as much as I like drawing. That's probably why I like making comics—you get to do both.

All of my comics are kind of about the same thing—a person having a superpower. I probably like writing them that way because of my own power. It's nothing amazing or exciting, and most people can't even see I have it, but it's there. It's an invisible power and those kinds of powers are harder to notice. My power is a secret. Mimi is the only one who knows about it, and she promised, *Cross my heart and hope to die,* never to tell anyone.

# WHAT EMPATHY POWER IS

Having empathy power means I am extra-sensitive to other people's feelings. When someone is sad or unhappy, I have to help him or her—no matter what. The *no matter what* part is the only not-good thing about my power. It sometimes gets me into trouble.

# MISS SUMMERS'S PROJECT

When Miss Summers described the project we were going to do, I could hardly believe it. It was perfect for me. It was a project with many parts, and I loved each one of them!

PART ONE OF THE PROJECT
Draw a picture of a character you would like to write about.

There were a few questions after she said just this first sentence. Robert Walters wanted to know if he could draw a toaster. I know Robert Walters, so I knew the toaster thing was a joke. As soon as he asked the question, about five people started laughing. In Robert's world that was a giant success. It wasn't hard to imagine what his brain was thinking.

I AM SO AWESOME AND FUNNY!

I thought Miss Summers might get mad, but she didn't, not even one bit. She just smiled and said, "Toasters can be mysterious—you never know what is going to pop out of them." Robert must have liked that idea, because he nodded, put his head down, and then started drawing right away. That was kind of a surprise—normally he's not such a good student.

The other person who had a hand up for a question was Sandra Orr. I knew what her question was before she even opened her mouth.

HER QUESTION IS GOING TO BE ABOUT A CREATURE THAT STARTS WITH A "U" AND ENDS WITH AN "N."

The whole class was probably guessing the same thing as me, because Sandra Orr is pretty predictable. Predictable means you can tell that something is going to happen before it happens—usually because it has happened a lot before. With Sandra Orr it was easy to predict her question because every time there is a project she asks the same thing.

CAN I DRAW A UNICORN?

PART TWO OF THE PROJECT

Part two of the project was my favorite part. Once we finished our drawings, Miss Summers was going to take them and shrink them down so they were small—so small that they could fit into a pocket. Then she was going to put clear tape on them to protect them and we were going to cut them out. This part was a little confusing, so she had to explain it a couple of times. Crafts aren't easy to explain with just words—that's why craft books have lots of pictures. It's easier that way.

① BIG DRAWING.

② DRAWING IS NOW SMALL.

MAKE THE DRAWING SMALL BY SHRINKING IT WITH THE PHOTOCOPIER.

③ DRAWING IS NOW COVERED WITH CLEAR TAPE.

YOU CAN'T TELL THE DIFFERENCE BECAUSE THE TAPE IS SEETHROUGH.

④ CHARACTER IS NOW CUT OUT.

HE'S SO CUTE!

# WHAT A POCKET PAL IS

It's what we are going to end up with when we are finished.

I loved the name "pocket pal." It made the project even more exciting. Who wouldn't want a pocket pal? There is always someone in our class who has to make trouble, so it wasn't a huge surprise when Owen 1 started talking without raising his hand.

Miss Summers was not as patient with Owen 1 as she had been with Robert Walters. She didn't say anything mean, but there was a difference in her face. Even though she was trying to hide it, I could tell that she was gritting her teeth. Mostly I knew that because listening to Owen 1 sometimes makes me do the exact same thing. If Owen 1 were smart, he would have noticed and kept his mouth shut, but Owen 1 is not smart. He kept on talking.

I was wondering what Miss Summers was going to do, because Owen 1 was already sitting at the front of the class. Would she move him farther away? To the hallway? To the principal's office? If it were my choice, I know exactly where I'd move him, but teachers probably can't do that kind of thing.

OWEN 1 SITTING IN THE MIDDLE OF THE FIELD.

I looked at Owen 1. He didn't look at all nervous. That's the kind of person he is—a person who doesn't know that certain words can equal trouble. If Miss Summers yelled at him, he'd probably be completely surprised. He wasn't like the rest of us, knowing that the yelling was about to happen. I looked back at Miss Summers, but instead of being mad like before, she was smiling. There is only one reason that a teacher changes from mad to happy so fast. Miss Summers had a plan!

# WHAT OWEN 1 SAID

Nothing. I think he was too surprised. Owen 1 is not good at crafts. If he made paper pockets, they were going to be terrible. No one was going to want to use them. Miss Summers didn't know this, but she'd just done the perfect thing to make everyone remember to wear clothes with pockets.

# WHAT HAPPENED NEXT

Miss Summers explained the rest of the pocket pal project.

# POCKET PAL PROJECT

1. We will carry around our pocket pal and show him/her our world.

2. We will try to imagine what it would feel like to be so small.

3. We will write a story from the point of view of our pocket pal (meaning we will pretend we are our pocket pal).

Miss Summers is smart. She knew that projects are not always easy to explain with just words, so she gave us some examples.

# WHAT MISS SUMMERS IS NOT

Good at drawing. Her pocket pal looked like one of Mimi's little brother's drawings, but she didn't care. She waved it around, had it talk in a silly voice, and made us all laugh. When it was finally time for us to start our character drawings, we were all pretty excited.

We'd been working for about five minutes when Miss Summers made another announcement. She had been walking around looking at everyone's drawings, and now she was stopped at Brian Aber's desk.

I'M SORRY, CLASS. I SHOULD HAVE TOLD YOU BEFORE, NO VIOLENT CHARACTERS.

NO VIOLENCE AT ALL.

Of course, the only people who made complaining groaning noises were the boys.

I thought it would be easy, but I had trouble thinking of what to draw. Sometimes this can happen when all you have in front of you is a blank piece of paper. All I could think of was Owen 1's toaster, and I couldn't draw that.

## HOW I FINALLY GOT MY IDEA

# WHAT HAPPENED AT LUNCH

I sat with Mimi and Grace F. and we mostly talked about Miss Summers. Grace F. was excited about her, because she said that Miss Summers had a lot more style than Miss Lois. She said she was going to keep track of Miss Summers's outfit each day, and then she showed us the drawing she'd done of today's outfit. Grace F. is really good at art. It's the kind of good that can make you feel a little bit jealous. I've practiced, but no matter how hard I try, I can't make my hand draw like she does.

GRACE F.'s DRAWING OF MISS SUMMERS.

# THE SAD AFTERNOON

I was hoping that Miss Summers would have our pocket pals all ready for us when we got back from lunch, but she didn't. She said we'd have to wait until tomorrow, and instead of doing anything else new and fun, we just did our regular work. Even though it was the same stuff we do every day—math, spelling, and worksheets—it somehow felt worse.

ORDINARY WORK FEELS WORSE WHEN YOU HAVE TO DO IT AFTER SOMETHING FUN.

## WALKING HOME

Mimi and I walked home with Sammy and Max. They weren't as interested as we were in making last memories about the walk home, so they finally left us and walked ahead, because we were being too slow. I wasn't expecting it, but last memories can be a little bit sad. That's probably why people talk more about first times—they're more exciting.

## WHAT HAPPENED WHEN I GOT HOME

Mr. Scruffers jumped all over me like usual. I put my stuff down and took her straight outside to play ball in the backyard. When your dog has been waiting for you to play ball with her all day, it's not fair to make her wait one second longer, even if you really feel like having a snack. Mr. Scruffers could probably play ball forever—she loves it that much. Sometimes I wonder what that would feel like, to love something so much you never want to stop doing it. It would be nice if Mr. Scruffers could talk—just for a day. Then she could explain it to me.

Sometimes when I am outside with Mr. Scruffers, Augustine Dupre, my downstairs neighbor, will come out to say hi. She lives in the fancy apartment in our basement

with her husband, Luke. They are both French. Augustine Dupre is a flight attendant, and Luke is a UPS delivery man. They both have jobs that make people happy.

If they ever had a team-up of their jobs, they could make people super happy.

I always like it when Augustine Dupre visits with me, so I kept looking at her door to see if she was going to come out, but the only thing I saw was Crinkles's tail under the bushes. He was lucky that Mr. Scruffers was busy with her ball. Chasing Crinkles is another one of her favorite things to do.

WHAT MR. SCRUFFERS DIDN'T SEE

CRINKLES'S TAIL

Even though Crinkles belongs to my neighbor Mrs. Luther, he loves Augustine Dupre more. He comes over to visit her all the time, and it's not easy for him because he has to get past Mr. Scruffers, but I guess true love is worth it.

Just as I was throwing Mr. Scruffers's ball for maybe the twentieth time, Mimi came bursting out my back door. Two seconds later she was standing next to me. Mimi can run fast if she wants to. "Guess what?" she asked. That kind of question is impossible to answer, so I said, "What."

53
• • • • •

Mimi was a lot more excited about this news than I was. I'm more of a drawer than a maker. She already had a whole list of things that she wanted to make.

I CAN MAKE LITTLE BAGS, HAIR BOWS, STUFFED CHARACTERS, COFFEE COZIES, BOWS, HEART PILLOWS, CAT PILLOWS, PUPPY PILLOWS, LADYBUG PINS, AND A BUNCH OF OTHER STUFF.

I tried to act excited, but Mimi knows me: She could tell I was pretending. I thought she'd be disappointed, but she was smiling. "I saved the best part for last," she said. I shrugged. "We get to keep half the money for ourselves!" Now things were different. Money was something to get excited about, especially since we were both saving up for the summer carnival. Mom and Dad were going to take us again. We'd gone last year, and it had been great. Tons of rides, great food, and lots of fun stuff to look at, but Mom only gave us five dollars to play the games. The games are one of the best parts, so this year Mimi and I were saving our money. We were going to win as many stuffed animals as we could carry—plus I had my secret wish.

## WHAT I WANT TO WIN

RAINBOW TAIL COZY KANGAROO

THE BEST STUFFED TOY EVER.

Now I was trying to think of things I could make too. "We should make a list," said Mimi. "Okay, I said. "Just five more throws for Mr. Scruffers." When I was done, we all went inside and had a snack—a dog cookie for Mr. Scruffers and chocolate chip cookies for Mimi and me.

# WHAT IS SURPRISING

Once you start thinking about it, there really are a lot of things you can make just by decorating. Mimi's list was huge, but I had one too. The only bad part was that we didn't have a lot of time. "I wish we'd known about this sooner," I complained. Mimi nodded and said, "We're just lucky we got it at all." I nodded and popped the last bite of my cookie into my mouth. Mimi was right. This was our lucky day.

# MY LIST

- DECORATE CUPS
- DECORATE NOTEBOOKS
- DECORATE JARS
- DECORATE PLATES
- DECORATE GLASSES

After our snack, Mimi went home to get all her supplies together and I went upstairs to make a list of all the things Mom needed to help me buy. I already had a plan in my head of how to convince her. Thinking about it made me smile.

MOM, IT'S FOR THE SWEET LITTLE CHILDREN AT ROBERT'S SCHOOL.

ME PRACTICING

TRYING TO MAKE IT SOUND REALLY IMPORTANT.

# WHAT HAPPENED AFTER DINNER

Mom took me shopping. We went to the craft store and the dollar store. I was a little surprised about how easy it had been to convince her. I was expecting her to say no. Maybe I suddenly had a superpower of mind control. I tried it out on the way home as we drove by The Big Scoop, my favorite ice cream place, but my powers were gone. She didn't stop.

By the time we got home, it was too late to start making anything, so I just organized it all. I like unpacking things from the store, especially when it's not groceries. Pretty soon all my new stuff was ready for tomorrow. I am happy to go to bed when there is something fun happening the next day—sleeping makes time go by faster. Tomorrow was going to be a great day. I just knew it. I flashed my light three times for Mimi and then got into bed. Mr. Scruffers jumped up like normal. She usually sleeps down at the bottom of the bed near my feet, but tonight I pulled her up close. If we cuddled, there would be room for everyone: me, Mr. Scruffers, and Rainbow Tail Cozy Kangaroo.

# WALKING TO SCHOOL

Usually Mimi comes to my house to get me, but today I was ready earlier than normal. I ran across my yard to her door, and this time I did not use the mail slot. Instead I just knocked. Mimi opened the door on my second knock. She was like me, excited, because she was ready to go too. Sometimes things can feel different even with only little changes, and we had two big ones—a new way to walk to school because of a new crossing guard, and a new teacher! When we got to the corner where we usually went straight, we both stopped. "This is it," said Mimi. This was the exact spot where our old way of walking to school ended and our new way of walking began. Today we were going to turn left.

I looked down the sidewalk at our old path and then stepped to the left. Mimi followed beside me and we were on our new route.

Up ahead I could see the crossing guard. Even from far away crossing guards are hard to miss. It's because of the super-bright clothes they have to wear.

"When we get there we should introduce ourselves," I said. "So the crossing guard feels welcome." "And shake his hand," said Mimi. "That's important too." Up ahead of us, a group of kids were already at the corner. I'd hoped that Mimi and I would be the first people to meet the new crossing guard, but I guessed that wasn't going to happen. Out of everybody, I wanted the new crossing guard to like us best.

### WHAT I IMAGINED IN MY HEAD

"Look!" said Mimi. She grabbed my arm. For a second I didn't know what she was talking about, and then I saw it. The crossing guard wasn't a man—she was a woman. I don't know why I'd never thought of that before, but I hadn't. It was a surprise, and a nice one.

As soon as we got close enough to talk to her, the crossing guard smiled and said, "Hi, girls." Mimi and I both said hi back at the exact same time, and then we introduced ourselves and shook her hand. The crossing guard didn't talk very much, but she said her name was Marie, and smiled again. She was older than I thought she would be—older than Mom, but not as old as a grandma. I wanted to ask her if it was fun to be a crossing guard, but we didn't have time. Once she stopped the cars for us, we had to walk to the

other side. When we got there, we waved
and shouted thank you.

# WHAT IS KIND OF IMPOSSIBLE

To have a conversation with someone when
you are standing across the street from them.
It was a little disappointing. I had lots of questions for Marie, and now none of them was
going to get answered.

"Maybe we can talk more on the way home," said Mimi. I nodded and smiled, because I knew just how to make that happen. I was going to make Marie a card—a Welcome to the Corner card.

Mimi and I got to school much earlier than normal, probably because we'd left early and the new walk was shorter. We had a whole ten minutes before the line-up bell was going to ring. Grace F. was talking to Jordan, so we went over and stood with them. Jordan is usually playing some kind of chasing game, so it was nice to get time to talk with her when she wasn't running. Grace F. was talking about Miss Summers and showing Jordan the sketch she had done of her outfit from yesterday. "I wish I were in your class," said Jordan. "Me too," I said. Jordan was fun to hang around with. It was too bad we couldn't trade people between classes. If that kind of thing could happen, I knew exactly who I'd trade to get her.

## WHAT HAPPENED IN CLASS

Miss Summers had our pocket pals all shrunk down, taped up, and waiting on our desks. It was exciting. I couldn't believe how cute my little squirrel looked. Miss Summers said if we wanted to, we could cut our characters out. Once I did that my squirrel was even cuter than before. All I wanted to do was play with him.

Other kids were liking their characters too, because soon there was lots of talking and moving around the classroom. When I looked over toward Mimi, I caught sight of Sandra Orr. She was making her unicorn pocket pal fly through the air. That was double imagination.

Miss Summers let us play around for a lot longer than I was expecting. It was hard to imagine Miss Lois letting us make all this noise. She's more of a regular old-fashioned kind of teacher.

# THE REST OF OUR
# POCKET PAL INSTRUCTIONS

1. Play with your pocket pals.
2. Imagine what the world must be like for them—they are so small.
3. Pretend you are your character. What are your feelings? Write them down.
4. Write a story.

Of course, everyone liked the number one part of the project the best, especially two boys who sit right near me.

YOUR DAYS ARE NUMBERED. YOU'RE TOAST!

GREEN BEAN MAN ISN'T SCARED OF YOU!

PREPARE TO BE TURNED INTO CRUMBS!

ROBERT WALTERS'S CHARACTER, ZOMBIE TOAST.

OWEN 1'S CHARACTER, GREEN BEAN MAN.

I wasn't sure if they were supposed to be fighting, but I didn't say anything. I'm not a tattletale kind of person—plus if they were busy with each other, then they weren't bugging me. Since Miss Summers was letting us move around, I went over to Mimi's desk. It was safer on her side of the room. There was less chance of being attacked by vegetables or a zombie.

Mimi's character was cute. She always says she can't draw, but that's not true. If she wants to and tries, she can do a pretty good job. Mimi held it up for me. "It's a sandwich," she said. "Her name's Sandy."

SANDY
THE
SANDWICH

Mimi picked up Sandy and made her dance around on her desk. "If we could start again, I'd draw something different," said Mimi. Sandy was cute, but it wasn't the kind of thing I'd expect Mimi to draw, especially when she could have picked anything. "Why a sandwich?" I asked. Mimi looked across the room and whispered, "It's Robert's fault. After he said *toaster,* all I could think about was food." I nodded. I knew exactly what she was talking about.

## WHAT MISS SUMMERS SURPRISED US WITH

Little mini notebooks to go with our pocket pals.

REGULAR-SIZED NOTEBOOK

MINI NOTEBOOK

Miss Summers said that lots of real writers carry around notebooks all the time. "You never know when an idea might come to you," said Miss Summers. "With this notebook, you'll always be ready to write it down." Miss Summers said that she hoped the notebooks and pocket pals would fit into everyone's pockets, but if they didn't, we could use one of the pockets Owen 1 had made.

I was right: Not one person asked for an extra Owen 1 pocket.

When it was lunchtime, Miss Summers said, "Do take your notebooks and pocket pals with you. Send your pocket pal down the slide, or go for a ride on the swing. Be adventurous, and don't forget to imagine yourself as your character. What is he or she feeling? And write down some notes. It'll be fun." We all said okay but the okay was only half true, because there probably wouldn't be notes. No matter how cheerfully someone says it, fun and notes do not belong in the same sentence.

## WHAT HAPPENED ON THE PLAYGROUND

There was pocket pal craziness everywhere. Owen 1, Robert Walters, and Brian Aber were all standing on top of the jungle gym dropping their pocket pals to the ground. If I had to write a note about their pocket pals' feelings, I knew exactly what I'd put down.

POCKET PAL FEELINGS: UPSET, SCARED, FEELING LIKE THE WORLD IS BEING TAKEN OVER BY CRAZY HUMANS.

Mimi and I didn't take our pocket pals to the slide or the swing, mostly because there were too many people already there. Instead we sat with Grace F. and Grace L. under the trees by the fence. "Maybe our pocket pals can be on a picnic," suggested Grace F. She had, of course, a perfectly drawn lady for her character. It was hard not to be jealous—at least a little bit. Grace L.'s character was a goat. I wanted to ask her why, but Mimi interrupted my thinking. She held her little sandwich in front of us and said, "Sandy can't go on a picnic! She'll be eaten." Suddenly we were all laughing. Mimi laughed too, even though she said she was trying to think like Sandy and if Sandy were real she would have been the opposite of happy.

After, when we finished laughing, we all decided to name our characters too. Grace F. and Grace L. were pretty quick about picking out names, but I had a hard time even deciding if my squirrel should be a boy or a girl. Some girls like only girl things, but I'm not

like that—sometimes I like boy things too.
It didn't help my concentrating when Grace
L. and Grace F. started playing with their
pocket pals. I tried, but Queen Veronica was
impossible to ignore, especially when she
started dancing and singing with Sweet Pea
the Third. They didn't care at all that I was
trying to do some thinking. Finally I just had
to close my eyes and cover my ears to block
them out.

It took a while, but right before the bell
rang to end lunch, I figured out my squirrel's name. It was Stan and it stood for Squir-

rel That's Always Naughty. When I first told Grace L., Grace F., and Mimi the name, I could tell that they didn't really like it, but after I explained that each letter stood for a word, they changed their minds. "Why did you pick naughty instead of nice?" asked Grace F. I knew that someone was going to ask me that, so I had the perfect answer all ready.

NAUGHTY IS MORE FUN TO WRITE ABOUT.

I'M FULL OF TROUBLE.

## OUR BORING AFTERNOON

When we got back from lunch Miss Summers said we could have ten minutes to write notes in our notebooks. She didn't ask, but somehow she knew that hardly anyone had done it at lunchtime. She said that those people who had already done their notes could read. I looked around and the only two people taking out their books were Marta and Sunni, but that wasn't a surprise—they're always perfect students. And then suddenly a thought popped into my head. Marta and Sunni were like good squirrels, and if they were good squirrels, who were the naughty squirrels? It took me only a second to decide. The number one naughty squirrel of the class was definitely Robert Walters. I hadn't thought about it before, but Stan and Robert Walters were kind of alike. Is that where I got the idea? Did watching Robert Walters make me think of Stan? I tried to imagine what Stan would be like if he were big and people-sized—would he and Robert Walters be friends? No, a giant squirrel was a lot scarier than a regular Robert Walters. Thinking that made me happy that our pocket pals were tiny. Big things were a lot scarier.

After the ten minutes of writing in our notebooks, Miss Summers had us put them away. I was not happy about that, because it meant exactly what I thought it was going to mean—now we had to do regular work. I guess that was our pattern until Miss Lois got back: fun mornings and boring afternoons.

## WHAT I WAS ABLE TO DO WITHOUT ANYONE SEEING ME

Make a fast card for Marie, the new crossing guard. Normally when I make a card, I draw things that the person I'm giving the card to likes, but with Marie, that was impossible. We didn't know anything about her, so instead I drew a picture of the street where we'd met her, and wrote, *Welcome to the corner*. I signed it and left a place where Mimi could sign her name too. I would have colored it, but that was too tricky with Miss Summers standing at the front talking to us. She would have for sure noticed me taking out all my colored pencils.

## WHO WAS HAPPIER THAN I WAS THAT SCHOOL WAS OVER

Mimi. "I just want to get home and start on the fair projects," she said. "Don't you? Do you want to come over?" "Good idea,"

I said, and while she signed the card, I told her about all the stuff Mom had bought me. And then I told her the best part: "And I didn't even have to beg for anything. You know my mom—usually it takes a while before she says yes, but this time it was so easy."

When Mimi looked up from signing the card, she was smiling. "It probably helped that my mom called your mom before I told you about the sale," she said. That was a huge surprise for me. No wonder it had been so easy.

## WHAT I WAS GLAD I DIDN'T SAY

IT WAS ALMOST LIKE I HAD A SUPERPOWER. THE SUPERPOWER OF MIND CONTROL.

MIMI LAUGHING BECAUSE SHE KNOWS THE TRUTH.

Even if you are with your best friend, who you trust 100 percent, you still don't want to feel dumb.

## HOW MARIE FELT ABOUT THE CARD

She loved it. She must have said thank you about ten times, and couldn't stop saying how happy she was. She said the minute she got home she was going to hang it on her wall. "Will you show your family?" asked Mimi. Marie was quiet for a moment, and then said that she lived alone. "I just moved here two months ago," she said. "When my son's finished with college, he's going to live here too. That's why I moved, to be closer to him." "When is that?" I asked. What Marie said next was a surprise. I was expecting her to say two weeks or a month, but her answer was a lot further away. "In a year," she said. I couldn't believe it—she had to wait a whole year to be with her family? "Well, it's good you have friends," said Mimi. Marie shook her head, but when she saw that we were getting sad she said, "But I'm not lonely, I have Freckles, my cat. I love cats." "Me too," said Mimi, "but I can't have one because I'm allergic."

After that, things got a little happier, and Marie talked about all the things she was looking forward to doing in our town. Some of it I didn't quite understand, but I smiled and nodded, because being polite is important, even if you are confused.

"What's an aviary?" Mimi shrugged—she didn't know either. I thought about that for a minute and then said, "I think she lied." Mimi stopped walking. "About the aviary? How do you know? We don't even know what it is." I shook my head and told Mimi what I was thinking.

"Don't worry," said Mimi. She pulled my arm and we started walking again. "She can make friends with the other crossing guards. They probably all get together and do stuff. Maybe they even have parties." Suddenly I felt better. Mimi's brain always thinks of things mine doesn't. She was right—I hadn't thought about the other crossing guards. Mimi let go of my arm and stopped pulling—she could tell I felt better. "Race you home," she said. I usually beat Mimi, but today I let her win. It was a secret thank-you for helping me be happy again.

I WIN!

# THE BEST THING ABOUT MAKING THING FOR A CRAFT FAIR

Making them with a friend. After playing with Mr. Scruffers for about half an hour, I packed up all my stuff and went over to Mimi's house. Mimi had already started sewing. She was in heaven. If there is something that Mimi's hands like to do more than sewing, I don't know what it is. At first I couldn't tell what she was making, but she explained it, and as soon as she did, I wanted her to make one for me, too.

I unpacked my paint pens. They were great. You could draw on glass, pottery, or even metal and your design would last forever—even in the dishwasher.

## THE BAD THING ABOUT THE DOLLAR STORE

Not everything costs a dollar. The first time I went into the dollar store, I got kind of mad about that. It was disappointing, like they were lying. The store was called Dollar Store, but when you got in there, a lot of the things were more expensive than a dollar. I thought Mom would be mad too—she hates it when people are tricky on purpose—but she wasn't. She said, "The Dollar Store can't help it. They can't change their sign every time prices go up. It would be too expensive." I'd never thought about that. Suddenly it all made sense.

A STRANGE NAME FOR A STORE

DOLLAR AND TWELVE CENTS STORE

## THE BEST THING ABOUT THE DOLLAR STORE

Even if things don't exactly cost one dollar, they are still not very expensive. It was the perfect place to buy stuff to decorate for the fair. My favorite three things that we had bought were cute jars with lids, plain yellow and white mugs, and some long, skinny white plates. The first thing I was going to decorate was a mug. I picked up a yellow one and got out a red marker. "How are you going to decorate it?" asked Mimi.

Mom and I had had a big talk about designs on the way home from the store. Mom said,

"If you want people to buy these, you'll have to decorate them with designs that people will like." I had been thinking about that, and I even made a list of things that were popular, things like flowers, birds, and cats, but there were other things that people liked too. They weren't the kinds of things that were easy to draw, but I had some ideas.

### WHICH TWO THINGS ARE THE HARDEST TO DRAW?

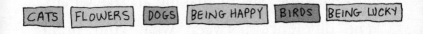

CATS  FLOWERS  DOGS  BEING HAPPY  BIRDS  BEING LUCKY

## WHAT IS NOT EASY TO PAINT

The inside of a mug. It's like trying to paint inside a very small tunnel. My big idea was that when the person who was drinking out of the mug finished their drink, they would see a message. It would be a fun surprise.

The first mug turned out terrible. You could hardly read what I'd written.

WHAT I WANTED THE INSIDE OF THE MUG TO LOOK LIKE

WHAT THE INSIDE OF MY MUG LOOKED LIKE

TODAY IS YOUR LUCKY DAY

TOP VIEW LOOKING DOWN

That's the part of making art that I hate. The difference between what your brain wants something to look like and what your hands can do. It makes me want to shout at my hands!

HANDS, I'M REALLY DISAPPOINTED IN YOU! YOU HAVE TO DO A BETTER JOB!

In the end, to fix the mug, I had to just paint the whole inside bottom of the cup red. I was about to try again with a new mug when Mimi stopped me. "Maybe there are too many letters," she said. "That's why it's hard—they can't all fit." She was probably right, but how could I say my message with fewer words? I put the cup down and tried out a few things in my head to see if I could make it shorter.

And then I had it. I picked up the cup and started writing. This time, it turned out much better. I said one out-loud thank-you and two silent thank-yous. "Thank you, Mimi." *Thank you, brain. Thank you, hands.* Mimi was the only one who answered back. She said, "You're welcome."

I still had to decorate the outside, and it took longer than I thought it would. Doing a good job of drawing is not something you can do fast. When I was finally finished, I handed it to Mimi so she could look it over. She loved it! "I want one," she said. "I'll use it for my orange juice. That way every day can be lucky." "Keep it!" I said. "I'll make more."

And then Mimi gave me the little bag she had just finished. It was so cute—she even put a flower on the front of it.

I felt like things were going well, but when I looked up at Mimi's clock, it was already time to go home. Maybe things weren't so good after all. I had a new bag, Mimi had a new cup, and for the fair we had . . . nothing!

WE'LL MAKE MORE STUFF TOMORROW, BUT NEXT TIME WE WON'T GIVE EACH OTHER PRESENTS.

We made a pinky swear so it would be official. It wasn't easy to do crafts with Mimi. I loved everything she made, but maybe that was a good thing. If I loved them, maybe other people would love them too. And who knew—maybe they'd love them so much that we'd sell out of everything in just minutes. I smiled about that all the way home.

# SAYING GOOD NIGHT TO MIMI

When I flashed my lights for Mimi, I held up the little bag she'd made me. I put all my favorite necklaces in it. When I looked across at Mimi, she was holding something too. It was my cup. Why did she have the cup in her bedroom? Maybe she loved it so much,

CUP SLEEPING ON ITS PILLOW NEXT TO MIMI.

she was going to sleep with it. Thinking about that made me laugh out loud.

# THE FIRST THING I THOUGHT ABOUT THIS MORNING

Marie. Even after everything Mimi had said, I was still worried. She was lonely, I just knew it. Cats are nice, but no matter how cute or furry or cuddly they are, a real human friend is better.

SO WHAT SHOULD I DO?

MEOW.

When Mimi came to get me, I was ready to go. I grabbed my backpack and headed out the door. I didn't say anything about my Marie feelings, but as soon as Mimi heard me asking Marie my questions, she was going to figure out what I was worrying about. Mimi is smart.

Even though this was only the second day of walking the new way to school, it already felt normal and not special like it had yesterday. It was surprising how fast things went from new to normal. As soon as we turned the corner, I saw Marie up ahead.

"Guess what?" asked Mimi. I asked her what back. She smiled and threw her hands in the air. "Today's my lucky day!" For a second I didn't get it, but then I remembered my lucky cup. She'd used it! "It was still fun," said Mimi. "Even though I knew what it was going to say." I nodded and then told her what I'd put in the bag she gave me. That made her happy too. When we got to the corner with Marie, we were both smiling. Marie was nice about answering my questions, but I was not happy to find out that all her answers were the same.

When we said goodbye to Marie, two things were different. Mimi and I had lost our smiles—we were sad. I had been right: Marie was lonely and alone. There was only one thing to do. "We have to help her find some friends," I said. Now Mimi looked even sadder than before. "That's too hard," she said. "We don't know anything about her, or even what kind of people she likes." Right after Mimi said that, I got the start of an idea. I didn't know how to finish the idea, but the start part was easy.

For a second I was worried that Mimi might say no and just want to keep walking to school, but she didn't. Instead, she turned around and said, "OK, but only five minutes, because I don't want us to be late."

# WHAT WE FOUND OUT ABOUT MARIE

I kind of had to tell Marie why I was asking her so many questions. Otherwise she would have been suspicious. But I didn't tell her everything. I couldn't—I didn't have a whole plan yet.

# WHAT IS KIND OF AMAZING

How much you can find out about a person in only five minutes. Mimi said it was because I asked good questions, but I don't think she was 100 percent right. I think it was more that Marie was happy to have someone to talk to. Freckles probably wasn't much good for that kind of thing.

## THE THINGS WE LEARNED
## ABOUT MARIE

MARIE LIKES

- BIRDS, ESPECIALLY OWLS
- THE COLOR YELLOW
- FLOWERS
- CATS
- TRAVELING— SHE'S BEEN TO PARIS, GERMANY, AND TEXAS
- FOOD — HOT DOGS, PANCAKES, AND POPCORN

- PLAYING THE FLUTE
- ALL PIES EXCEPT PUMPKIN
- FUNNY STORIES
- CUTE CHARACTERS
- MUSIC

We were lucky—we got to school just in time. As soon as we got to the playground, the line-up bell rang. Mimi and I walked toward class. "What are you going to do with what she told you?" asked Mimi. "Do you know someone for her to be friends with?" I shook my head, then answered her. "I don't have a plan yet, but . . ." Mimi interrupted me. "You'll think of something," she said. "You always do." I nodded like of course she was right, but my insides were not so sure.

## WHAT WE DID IN THE MORNING

More of the pocket pal project. Miss Summers sure loves that project. She let us play with our characters for almost an hour. It was kind of like no work, except for the having-to-take-notes part.

# WHAT STAN LIKES

I'd never made notes about a character before, but Miss Summers said it was a great way to find out our character's personality. She said, "Once you know their personality, it will be easy to write about them, no matter what kind of story they are in." After the hour was up Miss Summers made everyone go back and sit down. I was worried that we might start our boring afternoon work early, but that didn't happen. Instead, Miss Summers had us help her make a list of the different story types. I was glad we didn't have to copy them down—she just wrote them out on the whiteboard.

I had two good suggestions that were right. It always feels good to give a right answer and have the teacher write your words on the board.

MYSTERY AND SCIENCE FICTION.

HA! I WAS RIGHT.

I was a little surprised that Sandra Orr didn't say fantasy, because she loves unicorns so much, but then I remembered that she believes that unicorns are real. I don't know how she could think that, but she does. Mom says that sometimes people just believe what they want to believe—I guess Sandra is one of those.

When the list was finished, I knew what was going to happen next: Miss Summers was going to ask us to pick a story type for our writing project. Even though I'd said mystery and science fiction, I was going to pick something different. I was picking comedy.

## WHAT SOMEONE WHO DIDN'T KNOW KIDS WOULD THINK

That it would only take a few minutes for everyone to decide what kind of story they were going to write.

## WHAT I KNEW

It was going to take a lot longer. I was right—it took the whole rest of the morning. If I were Miss Summers, I would have been starting to get a headache. Too many questions and too much confusion.

# THE THING THAT HAPPENED DURING LUNCH THAT WE DIDN'T SEE

Miss Summers changed her mind about everyone learning the names of what to call different stories. She said it didn't matter if we got the names right or not because all she wanted us to know was that we had lots of choices. I'm not sure if having lots of choices was a good thing, because it took almost another hour for everyone to choose what kind of story they were going to write. I didn't mind, though, because sitting around waiting was a lot better than doing regular afternoon work.

IF PEOPLE KEEP ASKING QUESTIONS, WE'LL USE UP THE WHOLE DAY.

While everyone was busy picking out story ideas, I was busy too, but in a different way. I kept looking at Marie's list, hoping I could figure out what to do with it. It was kind of like a shopping list for a new friend, but friends aren't like groceries—you can't just go buy one at the store. Mostly I was wishing I knew someone who liked all the things Marie did—that would be perfect—but I didn't.

## WHAT WAS GREAT ABOUT THE REST OF THE AFTERNOON

Miss Summers said there wasn't time to do our regular work. So instead, we took out our pocket pals and played with them, and made notes for our stories, until the bell rang. I was really getting to like Stan. Naughty characters are fun! As soon as I thought that, I covered my mouth and looked over at Robert Walters. Did that mean I would now like Robert Walters? That we should be friends? This was not something I wanted to be true.

Sometimes a list can help your brain get unconfused. It seems strange that your very own brain, in your very own head, would be hard for you to understand—but it happens.

I decided to make the list in my tiny notebook. It kind of had something to do with Stan, so I decided it was okay, and it was faster than getting out a new piece of paper. A confused brain is not something you want to walk around with—it needs to be fixed as soon as possible!

| STAN | ROBERT WALTERS |
|---|---|
| SQUIRREL | HUMAN (AT LEAST ON THE OUTSIDE) |
| NAUGHTY | NAUGHTY |
| TINY-SIZED | NORMAL-SIZED |
| DOES THINGS WRONG | DOES THINGS WRONG |
| CAUSES TROUBLE | CAUSES TROUBLE |
| CONTROLLED BY ME | CONTROLLED BY HIMSELF |
| ANNOYING TO OTHERS | ANNOYING TO OTHERS |

# WHAT WAS GOOD ABOUT MY LIST

Robert Walters and Stan were almost exactly the same except for three things.

1. Stan was a squirrel and Robert Walters was human.
2. Stan was tiny and Robert Walters was big.
3. Stan was controlled by me, and Robert Walters was controlled by himself.

The list made me feel better. Those were three pretty big differences. It was proof that there was only one way for Robert Walters and me to be friends.

# WHAT WAS A TOTAL SURPRISE

Sammy's pocket pal. I hadn't seen it before, but now that I was looking at it, I couldn't believe it. I would have never guessed it in a million years. It was proof that people you know can still totally surprise you.

Sammy likes strange things, so I would have not been at all surprised if his pocket pal was something weird.

POCKET PALS THAT I WOULD EXPECT SAMMY TO MAKE

TALKING DIRT.

SLIME.

BUG WITH FOURTEEN LEGS.

# THE POCKET PAL THAT SAMMY MADE

Even though we were supposed to stay at our desks, I snuck over to Mimi's desk. Sandy the sandwich was in front of her, and Mimi was writing notes in her notebook. She smiled when she saw me. She would not have done that if Miss Lois were at the front of the class, but Miss Summers was different, we both knew. She wasn't going to get mad at us.

Mimi thought that I had come over to see her, but she was wrong—it was Sammy I wanted to talk to. Sammy's desk was close to Mimi's, and I had a question I needed him to answer. I reached over and poked him on the arm. When he turned around, he was surprised to see me. I pointed to his pocket pal. "Why did you make a cat?" I asked. "You hate cats." For a second Sammy didn't say anything, and then he answered.

## SAMMY'S ANSWER

I nodded and snuck back to my desk. Mimi must have thought I was being strange because I didn't stay and talk to her. Sometimes when your brain has to think, you just can't do chitchat.

WHAT MY BRAIN WAS THINKING

SAMMY AND I BOTH PICKED THE SAME KIND OF THING.

WE PICKED SOMETHING WE DON'T LIKE.

SQUIRREL WHO ACTS LIKE ROBERT WALTERS.

## BEING FRIENDS

Sammy's answer made me think two things about being friends.

1. Sometimes friends think alike.
2. Not all friends like the same things.

And then suddenly, I thought of more ways to find a new friend.

YOU MIGHT PICK A FRIEND BECAUSE...
- THEY SOLVE PROBLEMS LIKE YOU DO.
- THEY DON'T LIKE THE SAME THINGS YOU DON'T LIKE.
- THEY ARE INTERESTING TO YOU.
- THEY ARE FUNNY.

Now I knew what was next: To find Marie a friend, I needed more information. I needed to be like a detective and learn everything about her. I was glad that I'd only used half my mini notebook for Stan—the rest could be notes about Marie. Now I was extra excited for the bell to ring. Marie was only 246 steps away. I knew that because Sammy had counted them.

# WHAT MIMI THOUGHT OF MY NEW PLAN

Normally Mimi is pretty good about being excited with me when I have a plan because of my empathy feelings, but this time was different. Instead of saying something like, *Wow, Grace, that's a great idea,* she said, "What are you going to do with extra information? I don't know if you can really help her." Sometimes, if you are feeling really good about something, your good feeling will still stay with you even if someone doubts you. Today I was lucky—it was one of those times.

## SOMEONE SAYS SOMETHING YOU DIDN'T WANT TO HEAR

THAT'S OKAY. I'M STILL HAPPY.

NOW I FEEL SAD.

LUCKY DAY

NOT LUCKY DAY

"That's okay," I said. "I'll just ask the questions." Now instead of me looking sad, Mimi was looking sad. For a long while she didn't say anything—not even when I was asking Marie all sorts of new questions and writing down her answers. But then right before we got to my house, all the thoughts that were in Mimi's head came out at once.

YOU'RE GOING TO BE TOO BUSY WITH THE MARIE PROJECT TO DO THE CRAFT THING, AREN'T YOU?

I REALLY WANTED TO DO IT WITH YOU.

## WHAT I WANTED TO DO

Go home and write out everything about Marie on a big sheet of paper so I could see it all at once.

# WHAT I HAD TO DO

Shake my head and tell Mimi that she was wrong, and that what I wanted to do right now was work on the fair crafts. Sometimes even if you don't feel like it, you have to put the things you should do in front of the things you want to do.

## WHAT MIMI DID NEXT

Smile. "Okay," said Mimi. "Come over after you play with Mr. Scruffers." Mimi knows that no matter what, playing with Mr. Scruffers is always first on my lists of things to do when I get home.

THAT'S RIGHT. SHE CAN'T FORGET ABOUT ME.

## WHO CAME OUTSIDE WHILE I WAS PLAYING WITH MR. SCRUFFERS

Augustine Dupre. I am always happy to see Augustine Dupre. Mr. Scruffers is too, but not as much as I am. After barking and a few pets, Mr. Scruffers was ready to go back to playing ball. I was lucky that I could do both things at once—play ball with Mr. Scruffers and talk to Augustine Dupre. When Augustine Dupre asked me what was new, I told her all about Marie, including all the things that Marie liked. I crossed my fingers behind my back and hoped that Augustine Dupre would tell me one of the two things I wanted to hear.

### WHAT I WANTED TO HEAR

I HAVE THE PERFECT FRIEND FOR MARIE.

I KNOW HOW YOU CAN FIND MARIE A FRIEND.

# WHAT AUGUSTINE DUPRE SAID

Augustine Dupre always has good ideas, so even though she wasn't saying the exact things I wanted her to, I listened and tried not to look disappointed—plus now I kind of knew what an aviary is. Augustine Dupre likes talking, so she told me how her husband, Luke, was taking her out on a special date. She said she got a better job at the airline, so they were going out to celebrate. Augustine Dupre is a flight attendant in first class. That's almost at the front of the plane,

so it was kind of hard to imagine what a pro-
motion would be. The only place closer to
the front was the pilot job. Was that her new
job?

ARE YOU GOING TO FLY THE PLANE?

For a second Augustine Dupre looked surprised, and then she laughed and hugged me.
Normally when someone laughs at a question you ask, it can make you feel bad and
embarrassed, but Augustine Dupre knows
how to do it just right. If you add a hug, it
changes everything. I didn't feel one bit bad.
When Augustine is extra happy, or excited,
she always speaks in French. She squeezed

my shoulders and said, "Tu est drôle." I didn't know what she was saying, but it was something good, because she was smiling.

Finally she told me, "It means, 'You're funny.'" And then she told me all about her new job.

I'M GOING TO DO SOME TEACHING, SO I WON'T HAVE TO FLY TO FRANCE AS MUCH.

THAT WAY I CAN STAY HOME WITH LUKE.

Her new job didn't sound as fun as her old job. Flying to France sounded amazing, but that was probably because I'd never done it. After you've done something more than one hundred times, it's probably not so exciting anymore. We talked for a long time, and then

I suddenly remembered Mimi. She was waiting for me.

## WHO WAS SAD THAT I HAD TO LEAVE

Mr. Scruffers and Augustine Dupre. But I had to do it. I ran upstairs, got all my stuff, and then raced over to Mimi's house. As soon as I got to Mimi's door, she opened it. "I was waiting for you," she said, "and it wasn't easy." When I walked into the house, I smelled why. I followed Mimi and my nose to the kitchen. Mimi's mom makes the best banana bread in the world, and her whole house smelled delicious! The bread was waiting for us on the kitchen table, and not one slice had been eaten.

I looked at Mimi. "I'm so sorry," I said. I tried to explain about Augustine Dupre, but Mimi waved her hand to make me stop. "Sit down," she said. "I'm starving."

# THE TRUE FRIEND FRESH-BAKED
# BANANA BREAD TEST

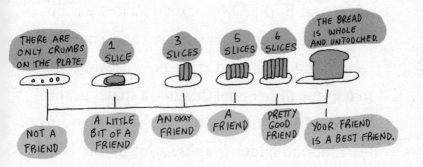

After eating, Mimi and I took out our supplies and started working. I worked on my cups and Mimi made some bags, and this time we didn't give each other any of them. Listening to music and working next to Mimi was fun, and we worked right up until it was time for dinner. The only time we stopped was to have dancing breaks, because when a good song is playing, it's almost impossible to stay sitting down.

# WHAT I DID AFTER DINNER

I went up to my room and took out all my Marie notes. I'm not very excited about a lot of the stuff that Miss Lois teaches us, but sometimes she'll surprise me and show us something cool. And right now, I was going to use one of her cool things—a spider graph. When Miss Lois first said we were going to learn about spider graphs, a lot of the boys got excited, and a lot of the girls got scared. I'm not a fan of spiders, so I was one of the scared people.

I DON'T LIKE SPIDERS.

ME NEITHER.

YAY! FINALLY WE GET TO LEARN ABOUT SOMETHING COOL.

# THE FIRST BEST THING
# ABOUT SPIDER GRAPHS

They have nothing to do with real spiders. When Miss Lois told us that part, it was a huge relief, and it made Abigail Whitkin get right down off the chair she was standing on. And then Miss Lois showed us a spider graph.

# THE SECOND BEST THING
# ABOUT SPIDER GRAPHS

Miss Lois was right: It makes understanding and learning things easier. When Miss Lois said the word *learning,* everyone in class groaned, but that was before we knew that spider graphs were kind of like putting drawing and learning together. If drawing is in the same sentence as learning, it definitely makes learning more fun.

I had a lot of notes about Marie. A spider graph was going to make them easier to understand—plus it would be kind of fun to make.

I took out a huge piece of paper and got started. The other fun thing about spider graphs is that the end is always a surprise.

You don't know exactly what it will look like
until it is finished.

## SPIDER GRAPH OF MARIE

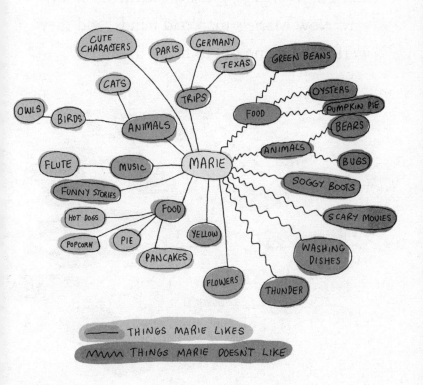

When I was done, I stood back and looked at it. Each branch looked kind of like an arm reaching to the world, and the circles were like hands. Normal spider maps probably don't have fingers, but I drew them on anyway. Now Marie's map had hands, and they were all reaching out to find a friend.

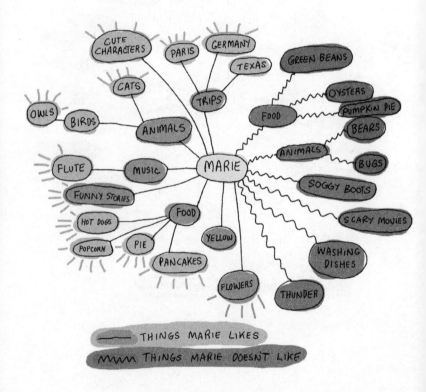

# WHAT IS HARD WORK

Making a spider graph. When it was bed-time, I was happy to go to sleep. My brain was tired. I flashed my lights to Mimi, but she wasn't in her room. This was easy to tell, because she didn't flash back. Normally when this happens, I wait a while and then try again, but tonight I was too tired. I just went straight to bed.

# WALKING TO SCHOOL

As soon as I saw Mimi, she asked me why I'd missed flashing my lights to her. She was a lit-tle bit upset, but after I explained that I hadn't forgotten, she felt better. I told her about my spider graph, but she wasn't very ex-cited. Sometimes it's hard to be excited about something when you are just talking about it and it's not there in front of you to look at.

When we got to the corner, we didn't cross the street right away, because Marie had a story to tell us about Freckles. She is good at telling stories.

LAST NIGHT WHILE I WAS IN BED I HEARD A STRANGE SWISHING SOUND.

IT SOUNDED LIKE WATER, BUT IT WASN'T RAINING OUT, SO I GOT UP TO INVESTIGATE.

THE NOISE WAS COMING FROM THE BATHROOM. I CREPT FORWARD AND CAREFULLY OPENED THE DOOR ... JUST IN TIME TO SEE FRECKLES FALL RIGHT INTO THE TOILET!

BOY, WERE WE BOTH SURPRISED.

# HOW TO TELL IF SOMETHING IS A GOOD STORY

You laugh until you cry, or until your stomach hurts. Marie's story made me do both, and we were still laughing and talking about it when we got to school.

# WHAT IS NOT AS FUNNY

Answering the question "Why are you laughing" by saying, "The crossing guard told us a funny story about her cat falling in the toilet." Telling the story with those words does not make people laugh. It just makes them say, "Oh."

## WHAT WAS NOT A GOOD SURPRISE IN CLASS

Miss Summers switched the fun and not-fun parts of our day around. Instead of working on pocket pals in the morning, we had to work on our regular boring stuff instead. "We'll save the best for last," said Miss Summers. I didn't say anything, but my brain was not thinking the same thing as hers.

NO FAIR! I WANT THE BEST NOW!

# LUNCHTIME

Mimi and I sat by ourselves because Mimi wanted to talk about all the things we still had to do for the fair. It was a lot more stuff than I was expecting. We were going to be working all weekend. If I were a give-up type of person, I might have said, *Forget it, it's too much work,* but instead I imagined Rainbow Tail Cozy Kangaroo sitting on my bed and said, "We can do it."

### MIMI'S LIST OF THINGS WE NEED TO DO

WE NEED TO MAKE POSTERS FOR THE SALE.

WE NEED SIGNS TO DECORATE OUR TABLE.

WE HAVE A LOT TO DO.

AND WE NEED TO FINISH ALL OUR CRAFTS.

# WHAT CAN SPEED BY SUPER FAST AND IS NOT A PLANE

An afternoon in class, if you are doing something you love, and I loved writing about Stan. I never noticed this before, but when I'm writing I make lots of faces. I was lucky that no one noticed me.

### FACES I MAKE WHILE WRITING

HAPPY  ANGRY  SURPRISED  UPSET

When the bell rang at the end of the day, I could hardly believe it. Miss Summers said we could finish our stories on Monday, which was good news for me, because Stan was caught in a trap, and that wasn't a good way to end a story.

HEY, YOU CAN'T LEAVE ME IN HERE ALL WEEKEND.

# WHAT WAS DISAPPOINTING

How long it took to decorate my stuff for the fair. As soon as school was over, Mimi and I rushed home, and after throwing the ball for Mr. Scruffers, I went straight over to Mimi's house. It was almost dinnertime, and so far I'd only decorated three things. It was hard not to be disappointed, because we'd worked the whole entire time, without even one single dancing break. When you do that much work, you expect a giant pile of stuff—not just three cups.

# WHAT I COULDN'T STOP THINKING ABOUT

The spider graph and how I wanted to show it to Mimi, but that wasn't going to happen, because I'd left it at home. I'd been in such a hurry that I'd forgotten to bring it over. Sometimes you can know things about other people, and right now I knew that if I went home to get the spider graph, Mimi would be mad. She was being a lot like Miss Lois, only instead of talking about school stuff, she was talking about fair stuff.

# WHAT IS NO FUN

When your best friend starts turning into your teacher. I was glad when Mimi's mom called us down for dinner. During dinner, Mimi turned back into herself. This was a relief. It was a lot more fun to be sitting next to regular Mimi instead of Mimi on the outside and Miss Lois on the inside. "Do you know what I want to win at the carnival?" she asked.

I guessed a giant panda, but I was wrong, and then she surprised me with her answer. She wanted Rainbow Tail Cozy Kangaroo too. My first feelings were not happy ones.

But Mimi changed my feelings with what she said next.

Twinsies! It was a great idea.

# WHAT I WAS GLAD ABOUT

After dinner, instead of doing more work, we watched TV. Our favorite show, *Unlikely Heroes,* was on, and it was an episode that we hadn't seen before. *Unlikely Heroes* is a good show for three reasons.

1. All the stories are 100 percent true.

2. It's a show about helping people when they are in trouble.

3. Sometimes people get teeny-tiny super-powers, right when they need them.

Tonight, my favorite part of the show was when they interviewed the teenager who had saved a mom and her little girl from a bear.

After the show I could tell that Mimi wanted to do some more work, but her mom said we had to play a game with Robert instead. I pretended to be disappointed, but on the inside I was glad. Mimi's mom said it wasn't fair for Mimi to ignore Robert, and that he needed her attention too. What she was saying reminded me of what Mom had told me about Mr. Scruffers.

# WHAT DOES NOT WORK WITH ROBERT

Card games. What Robert says about cards:

1.  There are too many to hold.
2.  I can't remember them all.
3.  I don't know which one goes with which one.
4.  I don't want to play!

# WHAT TOOK TEN MINUTES

Picking up the cards Robert had thrown all over the house. We ended up going outside and playing catch. It made me smile—maybe Robert and Mr. Scruffers weren't so different.

When it was finally time to go home, I was exhausted! Mimi was not. As I was walking home she shouted at me, "Come over early tomorrow so we can make more stuff." I waved at her but didn't look back.

# WHAT I WAS HOPING

1. That tomorrow I would be filled with some of Mimi's crafting energy.
2. That Rainbow Tail Cozy Kangaroo was going to be worth it.

# WHAT I NEEDED FOR BREAKFAST

French toast. I always ask Mom to make me French toast when I need extra energy, or if I'm using my empathy powers. I don't know why it helps, but it does, and today I definitely needed extra energy. I was lucky that it was a weekend, because getting Mom to make French toast on a Saturday is a lot easier than getting her to make it on a school day.

# WHAT SHE SAYS ON A SCHOOL DAY

IT TAKES TOO LONG. HERE'S A MUFFIN.

After French toast and cleaning up my room and folding my clothes, I grabbed the spider graph and went over to Mimi's house. Room cleaning and clothes folding are not things I usually do unless Mom tells me to do them, but when you are looking for reasons to stay home, you'll do almost anything. Finally I had to go. When I knocked on Mimi's door, Robert opened it. He pointed upstairs and said Mimi was already busy. Normally

I'd say thank you and rush right up to Mimi's room, but today was different. Robert was holding a ball, so I put down my graph and stepped back so he could throw it to me. He was getting really good at catch and hardly ever missed, even the high throws. But I was still careful and didn't throw the ball very hard. We must have been making noise, because after about five minutes, Mimi came downstairs to see what we were doing.

ROBERT, GRACE CAN'T PLAY WITH YOU ANY MORE. SHE HAS TO WORK.

This was not good news. The Miss Lois Mimi was back!

# THE FIRST THING I DID WHEN I GOT UPSTAIRS

I showed Mimi the spider graph.

# WHAT SHE SAID THAT I WAS NOT EXPECTING

"I can't believe you did all that, and it wasn't even for school. That must have taken forever. Why did you do that?" For a second I didn't answer. This is a normal thing to do when someone has surprised you with a question. Mimi's words did not make me happy, but I ignored my upset feelings and pointed to the hands on the graph—that was my favorite part. I just had to make Mimi understand. "See these," I said. "They're like Marie's hands reaching out, and each one of these things is a way she could meet a friend."

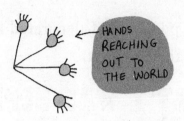

HANDS REACHING OUT TO THE WORLD

Mimi nodded. "So how are you going to find people who like those things?" Mimi's question was not a surprise, but still I couldn't answer it. I didn't have a plan. Mimi let me tape the map to her mirror so I could see it while we worked. I wasn't sure why, but I had the feeling the answer was on the graph—I just had to find it.

## WHAT MIMI AND I DID FOR THE WHOLE REST OF THE DAY

Make stuff for the fair, but this time we had lots of dancing, snacking, and playing-catch-with-Robert breaks. It wasn't my favorite Saturday in the world, but it wasn't as bad as I thought it was going to be, and by the end of it I had a pile of stuff decorated for the fair. That was the best part.

# WHAT I WAS HOPING

That on Sunday Mimi's family would be going on a trip somewhere.

## WHAT I WANTED TO HEAR MIMI SAY

I CAN'T WORK ON CRAFTS TODAY. WE'RE GOING OUT SOMEWHERE.

But Sunday was not my lucky day. Instead, Mimi came to get me before I'd even had breakfast. I was hoping for French toast again, but Mom is weird about making the same thing for breakfast two days in row. It doesn't make sense, but I couldn't convince her to change her mind, so she made pancakes.

## WHAT CAN HAPPEN WHEN YOUR DAY DOES NOT START LIKE YOU ARE EXPECTING IT TO

You can be a little bit grumpy.

I was still grumpy when we got to Mimi's house, and looking at my pile of decorated things did not make me feel better. It was big, but not as big as my pile of undecorated things. I flopped down on Mimi's bed like a starfish and didn't move. Maybe if I was super still and quiet, she'd forget about me.

## WHY I AM LUCKY

I have a smart, helpful friend. Today she was not at all like Miss Lois. She didn't say, "Get decorating—we need those things for the fair." What Mimi said was better.

DO YOU WANT TO MAKE A POSTER TO ADVERTISE OUR TABLE AT THE FAIR?

My answer to that was yes!

# WHAT I DID NOT KNOW BEFORE

Even though decorating things and making a poster are both drawing, they are not the same thing. This is why.

- Drawing one poster is fun and exciting.
- Decorating one cup is fun and exciting.
- Decorating nine more cups is boring.

Mimi gave me some paper and her markers, and I sat down to work. "What should I put on the poster?" I asked. "Just a minute," said Mimi, and she ran downstairs to see her mom. While she was gone, I stared at the spider graph and tried to make myself come up with an idea, but my brain couldn't think of anything. What if I never figured it out? What if I couldn't help Marie? These were thoughts I did not want to have, but they were there, in my brain.

I was glad when Mimi came back and interrupted my thinking. "Here," she said, and handed me a piece of paper. It had three things on it: the name, the address, and the time of the fair. "What else should I put on it?" I asked. Mimi thought for a moment and then answered. "Draw and describe the stuff we made. That way people who like those kinds of things will want to come."

For a second I didn't say anything. I just sat there frozen, and then I jumped up and hugged Mimi.

Mimi was surprised about both things—the hug and what I had said. I took a deep breath and then explained my idea. I was so excited, I could hardly get the words out fast enough.

FIRST I'LL USE THE LIST I MADE TO HELP ME DECORATE THINGS SO MARIE WOULD LIKE THEM.

THEN I'LL MAKE A POSTER THAT DESCRIBES ALL THOSE THINGS.

SO GUESS WHO WILL COME TO OUR TABLE AT THE FAIR? MARIE AND EVERYONE WHO LIKES THE THINGS THAT SHE DOES.

THAT'S HOW SHE'LL FIND A FRIEND.

## WHAT MIMI SAID

"I can't believe I helped you think of that." My brain was filled with ideas. As soon as I finished thinking about one idea, a new one would pop right in. "I'll make two posters," I said. "One will have all the things Marie likes on them, and the other one will be all our other stuff." Mimi smiled at me. She could tell things had changed—now I was filled with the same amount of fair energy as she was.

The first thing I worked on was making the poster for all our regular stuff. Mimi liked it so much, she promised to make something for the Marie project too.

## WHAT SURPRISED ME

Decorating things for the Marie part of the sale was a lot more fun than just decorating regular things to sell. I didn't want to stop for lunch, but when I smelled grilled cheese sandwiches, I put down my paint pen. It turned out to be a good idea, because Mimi's mom had made us an extra-delicious meal.

After we ate, Mimi and I went back to work, and by the end of the day, we both had pretty big piles of things to sell.

## SOME OF THE THINGS
## I MADE FOR MARIE

OWL CUP
ON THE OTHER SIDE IT SAYS "I OWLY HAVE EYES FOR YOU."

LONG SKINNY PLATE
CAT SLEEPING DECORATED WITH FLOWERS

DAD MADE THE HOLE IN THE LID FOR ME.
TRAVEL MONEY
JAR FOR SAVING MONEY TO GO ON A TRIP

PIE PLEASE
A FUN PIE PLATE

A PLATE DECORATED WITH CUTE FRUIT

NO BEARS
A CUP THAT SAYS "NO BEARS ALLOWED."

I still had to make the poster for Marie, but Mimi said I could do that tomorrow at school. Her mom wasn't taking her to get the posters photocopied until after school.

# WHAT CAN HAPPEN EVEN WITH BEST FRIENDS

After spending almost every minute of the whole weekend with your best friend, you might want to have some free time away. This does not mean you don't like your friend anymore; it just means you have friend overload. Both Mimi and I had it, because when I said I wanted to go home, she just smiled and said, "Good idea."

# WHAT I DID WHEN I GOT HOME

I made the poster for the Marie part of the sale. Even though I was tired, I had to do it. When I was done I took it to show Mom. She was impressed, and it wasn't just me thinking she was. She actually said it.

# WHAT FELT REALLY GOOD

Holding fifty copies of a poster that was going to find Marie a friend. I couldn't wait to show it to her.

## THE FIRST THING I SAID WHEN I SAW MIMI THE NEXT MORNING

"Look! I made the poster." I had three copies—one for Marie and then two extra ones. Mimi loved it, and was almost as excited as I was. Even though it was early, we left for school.

"Of course I'll come. How could I miss it? It has all my favorite things on it." On the way to school, I put up the other two posters. Now I couldn't wait for Wednesday night.

MARSHALL PRESCHOOL FAIR
~ TABLE 12 ~
OWLS  FLOWERS  CATS
PIE  POPCORN  HOT DOGS
PANCAKES  MUSIC  CUTENESS  TRAVEL
ALL IN ONE PLACE
WEDNESDAY 6 PM
618 NORTH WEBSTER STREET

PLUS THE POSTER HAS LOTS OF YELLOW ON IT AND THAT'S HER FAVORITE COLOR.

## WHAT WE DID WHEN WE GOT TO SCHOO

Mimi and I were extra early. We had a whole twenty minutes before the bell. The best view in the whole playground is the very top of the slide. Usually there are other kids already sitting there, but since we were early, we got there first. We sat down and looked around. Robert Walters and Owen 1 were running around with some other boys. It looked like some kind of chasing game, and Robert Walters was It. Mimi was watching too. "He'll never catch them," said Mimi. "They're too fast." Suddenly Robert Walters dropped to the ground. "Did he trip?" I asked. Mimi shrugged. "I couldn't tell," she said. Was he hurt? I stood up to get a better view. I wasn't the only one worried, because Owen 1 and all the other boys were coming back to look too. Suddenly Robert Walters jumped up, tagged one of the boys, and then ran away laughing. He'd tricked them. "Well, that's a surprise," said Mimi. "He's smarter than I thought he was." I nodded and said a silent thank-you, because it was the exact kind of surprise I needed for my story.

When the bell rang, Mimi and I lined up like usual. Normally I try to pay as little attention to Robert Walters as possible, but watching him for ideas for my character had changed things. It made him less annoying and a lot more interesting, and I was almost excited to see what he was going to do next.

## WHAT HAPPENED IN THE MORNING

Miss Summers had us finish writing our stories. She seemed a little more nervous than normal, but maybe that was because it was almost her last day. We were getting Miss Lois back tomorrow afternoon. I tried not to think about it.

Miss Summers was nice and let me put up my fair poster right in the classroom. I left room for Mimi so she could put hers next to it when she had copies. A lot of the girls said they were going to come, especially when Mimi told them she was selling headbands. She sometimes makes them and gives them away for birthday parties—all the girls that wear headbands really like them.

# WHAT HAPPENED IN THE AFTERNOON

Miss Summers made us rewrite our stories so they were nice and neat, and then if we finished early, she said we could draw a picture to go with them. It was my kind of afternoon, but it was not so much Robert Walters's or Owen 1's kind of afternoon. They did a lot of complaining.

HOW COME WE HAVE TO WRITE THE WHOLE THING AGAIN?

I DON'T WANT TO DO IT.

# WHAT HAPPENED AFTER SCHOOL

I went with Mimi and her mom to the copy store, and as a special treat on the way home, she bought us ice cream. "I'm really proud of how hard you girls worked," she said. "You deserve a treat." Parents don't say that kind of thing very often, so both Mimi and I were smiling. Plus the ice cream was extra delicious because Mimi's mom let us have two toppings.

After the ice cream, Mimi's mom walked around with us so we could put the posters in store windows. I was mad that I didn't have any of my special Marie posters with me, but Mimi said not to worry, that we'd come back. Mimi was right, because as soon as we got home, we ran over to my house to get Mom to take us back to the store. Mom said yes, so it was a double mom-duty day. It could have

also been a double frozen treat day, but Mimi
messed that part up.

## WHO SLEPT REALLY
## WELL ON MONDAY NIGHT

Me. Putting up posters was a lot more tiring
than I thought it would be.

# WALKING TO SCHOOL

Mimi and I were not early like yesterday. When we saw Marie we made sure she was still coming to the craft fair. She needed to be there for my plan to work.

# TWO SURPRISES

When we got to class all our stories and pictures were hanging up in the classroom. But that wasn't the best surprise. The best one was the fruit and bagel party we had at snack time. And apart from Owen 1 spilling juice all over his desk, everything went perfectly.

# ONE MORE SURPRISE

Sandra Orr surprised me by making a goodbye card for Miss Summers. Normally she's not an artist-type person. Of course the card had a picture of a unicorn on it, but it was cute, and she let everyone sign it. It was a nice thing to do.

We didn't do any work for the last twenty minutes before lunch. Instead, everyone was saying goodbye to Miss Summers. I was sad that she had to leave, and I wasn't the only one. Sandra Orr even cried. I guess that's why she made the card—she liked Miss Summers a lot. While everyone was busy with good-byes, Mimi put her poster up next to mine. They looked great together. If I weren't already going to be there, seeing the poster would make me want to go.

# LUNCHTIME

Mimi and I had lots to talk about at lunch: Miss Summers leaving, Miss Lois coming back, the craft fair, how we were going to decorate our table, and if my plan to find Marie a friend was really going to work. All that talking made time go by super fast. When the bell rang, we were both surprised that lunch was already over.

## WHO WAS THERE WHEN WE GOT BACK

Miss Lois, and she was not her normal self. She was smiley and happy, and didn't seem one bit upset that we hadn't done any math or spelling work yesterday. Not working on math and spelling would have been a good secret to keep, but someone told her about it. I wasn't sure who had done it, but I had my suspicions.

Even though Miss Lois was in a good mood, she still made us do math and spelling. She said we had some catching up to do. That was not a surprise, but just because you are expecting something doesn't mean you will be happy about it.

# WHAT HAPPENED AFTER SCHOOL

Mimi gave her extra posters to some of the teachers, and one of them even took two so she could put one up in the teacher's lunch-room. I was going to have to remember to bring one of my Marie posters for that to-morrow.

When we got home, Mimi and I made some signs for our table, and then we had to do the hard part—decide how much to charge for all our stuff. This was not an easy thing to do, so it was nice when Mimi's mom came to help us. She even had special little stickers for us to use as price tags. I didn't mind doing that part. I tried to count out how much money we would make if we sold everything, but I couldn't do it in my head. It made we wish I were a little bit smarter in math like Sunni was. I bet she could have done it.

SEE, MATH IS HELPFUL!

The last thing we did was pack all our stuff in boxes so Mimi's mom could take it to the fair. Tomorrow after school she was going to take us straight to Robert's preschool to set up our table. Then we were going out for pizza. After that—the fair would start! Thinking about it made me wish that tomorrow were today. When you are looking forward to something, it's not easy to wait.

# THE FAIR DAY

I woke up extra early, and the first thing I thought was *Today's the day!*. The second thing I thought was *I wish it weren't a school day*. Before school, I went over to Mimi's house to help put all our boxes into Mimi's mom's car. She offered to drive us to school, but I wanted to walk. I wanted to make extra sure that Marie was coming tonight.

# HE GOOD THINGS THAT HAPPENED TODAY

1. Marie said she was coming to the fair.
2. Miss Lois gave us a surprise spelling test. (This is not normally a good thing, but see number three to find out why this time was different.)
3. I got a great mark on my surprise spelling test.
4. Grace F. and Grace L. said they were for sure coming to the fair.
5. Miss Lois did not give us a surprise math test.

6. Mom gave me two cookies in my lunch. (I usually get one.)
7. Owen 1 did nothing to annoy me.

# THE BAD THINGS THAT HAPPENED TODAY

1. Miss Lois got mad at me for talking when I was trying to tell Sammy about the things Mimi and I had made for the fair.
2. Miss Lois got mad at me for talking when I was telling Marta she should come to the fair.
3. Miss Lois got mad at me for talking when I was asking Mimi if she thought we needed more signs for our table at the fair.
4. Miss Lois said I was not allowed to talk about the fair anymore until after school.

MISS LOIS IS NOT A LOVER OF CRAFT FAIRS.

# WHAT HAPPENED WHEN WE GOT TO THE FAIR

Robert's school was super busy, with people rushing around everywhere. Even though I'd been there before, I was glad that Mimi's mom was leading the way. The first thing she did was help us find our table. It was a lot bigger than I thought it was going to be. Mimi and I were worried about that, but Mimi's mom said if we spread our stuff out, she was sure we'd be able to fill it up.

## WHAT IS NOT EASY TO DECIDE

If we should put the Marie things all together in one place or if we should spread them out all over the table. We tried both, but I just couldn't decide.

### WHY HAVING THE MARIE
### THINGS IN ONE PLACE IS GOOD
The person who is standing and looking at them likes the same things that Marie does.

## WHY SPREADING THE MARIE
## THINGS OUT IS GOOD

It will keep the person at the table longer because they will have to find all the things they like.

I finally picked the spreading-it-out idea.

When we were all done with setting up our table, we were both really happy with it. Mimi's mom took some pictures of us standing behind it so we could remember it forever. It was pretty exciting.

## WHAT WAS EVEN MORE EXCITING

Having someone come by and actually buy two of our things. And it was perfect, because the lady bought something Mimi had made and something I had made. Mimi and I were putting all the money from the sale together, so it didn't matter how much we each sold, but still it was nice for both of us to be selling things. It meant that at the end of the fair I was not going to be sad or disappointed.

### WHAT I WILL NOT SAY

## WHAT WAS THE MOST EXCITING MOMENT

Seeing Marie walking toward us. She looked different without her crossing guard outfit on—less easy to recognize. Of course, she loved everything on the table. She said, "It almost looks like these things were made for me." I didn't tell her that she was right. Instead, I just smiled. Marie spent a long time looking at everything, and that was just perfect. All we needed to do was to keep her at the table until other people came by to look too.

## HOW THE PLAN WORKS

1. MARIE STAYS AT THE TABLE.

2. SOMEONE COMES ALONG WHO LIKES THE SAME THINGS AS SHE DOES.

3. THEY TALK, AND THEN BECOME FRIENDS.

4. TA DA! THE PLAN IS A SUCCESS!

## WHAT WAS NOT WORKING

My plan. There were lots of people coming to the table, but not any of them were talking to Marie. They were only talking to us. While Marie stood looking over our stuff, we sold six things, and two of them were even part of the Marie project! But not one single person talked to her.

## WHAT WAS HORRIBLE NEWS

Marie saying she was going to have to leave in a few minutes. This was a disaster! We couldn't let her go. We had to make her stay. Suddenly I knew how to do it.

I grabbed Mimi's hand and pulled her across the room with me before she could complain.

## WHO WAS MAD

Mimi.

THIS ISN'T FAIR! BEING AT THE TABLE IS THE FUN PART, AND NOW I'M MISSING IT.

The whole time Mimi was complaining, I was watching our table. Suddenly I grabbed Mimi's arm and pointed. She stopped talking. Now I was glad we weren't at the table, because standing there in front of Marie was

Miss Lois. Miss Lois was not someone I wanted to see if I didn't have to, especially after today. What was she even doing here? Mimi felt the same as me, because she changed her mind about being away from the table. She said, "Okay, you win. We'll stay here for a while, but as soon as Miss Lois leaves, we're going back."

# WHO DID NOT LEAVE

Miss Lois! She was totally ruining my plan. Marie wasn't talking to anyone but her. There were other people standing at our table, and

WHY WON'T SHE GO AWAY!

some even bought stuff, but none of that made Miss Lois leave. My feelings for Miss Lois were not good ones.

# WHAT WAS A SURPRISE

Miss Lois bought three things from our table. Mimi and I couldn't believe it. "Maybe we should go back," said Mimi. It was not what I wanted to hear, but she was right. We couldn't spend the whole fair hiding and pretending to go to the bathroom.

# WHAT FEELS BAD

Knowing that your plan is a 100 percent failure, especially if it took a lot of work—and mine did! Mimi and I walked back to the table. I tried to look happy to see Miss Lois, but it wasn't easy. My outside face and my inside feelings did not match up. Miss Lois did not have the same problem as me—she was 100 percent happy.

# WHAT IS IMPOSSIBLE TO DO

Stay mad at someone when they are being super nice to you, especially if they use words like *talented* and *amazing*. Marie seemed happy too. It was good that she didn't know about my plan, or she would have been like me, disappointed on the inside. I didn't want to give up on the plan. I wanted Marie to stay longer, but she looked at her watch and said, "I've got to get the bus back home. I know it's silly, but my favorite show is on—*Birds of the Wild.*" And then suddenly she and Miss Lois were talking again.

Mimi was too busy helping other people to pay attention to what was happening, but I was. I just stood there staring. I couldn't believe it. My plan was working, and it was happening right in front of me. Marie was making a friend.

After Marie and Miss Lois left, the rest of the fair was kind of a blur.

1. Grace F. and Grace L. came by, and they each bought one thing.
2. Sammy came by, and he didn't buy anything.
3. Mom came by and took lots of pictures.
4. Two other teachers from school came by.
5. Augustine Dupre and Luke bought four things, plus they brought us a snack—chocolate chip cookies! Augustine Dupre is the best!

Everything seemed like it was happening super fast, and before we even knew it, the fair was over.

## HOW YOU CAN TELL IF YOU HAVE HAD A SUCCESSFUL FAIR

You only have five things left on your table. Mimi's mom couldn't believe it. When all the money was counted up she said, "You made eighty-eight dollars and fifty cents!" That was the best news ever! We had to give half to Robert's school, but still that meant we had forty-four dollars and twenty-five cents for us.

I offered to give Mom some money to pay for the supplies she'd bought me, but she said, "No, thank you." So instead of money I gave her a big thank-you hug.

Things hadn't turned out exactly like I was expecting them to, but that kind of thing happens a lot in real life. Mostly I was lucky that the *turning out* was pretty close to what I wanted. When you can smile while you are thinking about something, that is a good sign. It was a surprise to me and something that I never could have guessed, but thinking about Miss Lois and Marie being friends made me smile.

# THE BEST NEWS EVER

# COZY KANGAROOS

The carnival wasn't going to be happening for a few months. That part was not good news, especially because I don't like waiting, but some things are worth waiting for—especially if you really, really want them. Mimi and I had three new words for flashing our lights: *We're coming, twinsies!*

WE'RE WAITING FOR YOU.